BILLY AND THE MINI MONSTERS

MONSTERS

Monsters Go Party!

ZANNA DAVIDSON

Illustrated by
MELANIE WILLIAMSON

Reading consultant: Alison Kelly

Meet Billy...

Billy was just an ordinary boy living an ordinary life, until **ONE NIGHT** he found five **MINI MONSTERS** in his sock drawer.

Gloop

Peep

Fang-Face

Captain Snott

Trumpet

Then he saved their lives, and they swore never to leave him.

We give you the Secret-Hairy-Snot-Tooth Oath of Devotion.

We're awesome!

And fun!

And SCARY!

Are we scary? I'm not sure I'm very scary.

One thing was certain — Billy's life would never be the same **AGAIN**...

Contents

Party!

Chapter 1
Party Time

Billy was
very excited.
It was his friend
Jack's birthday,
and he was going to
his costume party.

Unfortunately, his little sister Ruby was friends with Jack's little sister, so she was coming too.

But Billy found it very HARD to be nice to Ruby.

She destroyed his toys...

...ruined his games...

…and always wanted to play in his bedroom.

There was **NO WAY** Billy was going to let Ruby into his bedroom.

Ruby had to learn that Billy's bedroom was PRIVATE.

Because Billy had his
TOP SECRET
pets to protect.

The MINI MONSTERS!

"We can't wait to come to the party!" said Captain Snott. "I've been practicing the birthday song."

Happy Snottday to you, Happy Snottday to youuuuu...

Um, that's not how it goes.

The Mini Monsters had been busy dreaming about Jack's birthday party **ALL WEEK**.

"I'm sorry but you can't come to the party," said Billy. "Not after what's happened the last few times."

The Mini Monsters were always getting into trouble:

At the swimming pool...

Fang-Face and Captain Snott nearly drowning.

Gloop being SUCKED down the drain.

At home...

All of the monsters getting trapped in the washing machine.

At school...

Peep ending up in a hamster cage...

...and Trumpet sinking in a vat of baked beans.

And at the airport...

Gloop and Trumpet getting lost with the luggage.

Billy had caused so much trouble trying to rescue them he'd had **NO**
TV
FOR A
WEEK.

Billy knew if the Mini Monsters came to the party, he would end up in **EVEN MORE** trouble.

"I'll make it up to you," said Billy.
"I'll bring you back some cake!"

I want you to stay RIGHT here.

We promise.

"Bye," called Billy. And he went
out of his room, and shut the door.

16

19

Chapter 2
The Magic Show

Billy sat down with his friends.
There was going to be a magic show.

"Let the show **begin**!"
said the magician.

He magicked

FLAMES

from his
wand…

…made amazing
balloon animals…

…and even sawed the birthday boy in half.

Don't worry - I'll put him back together.

"And now for my final and favorite trick – the rabbit in the hat!" the magician said.

The magician tapped his hat
three times...

one

two

three

Then he put his
hand **inside**...

and pulled out...

23

Chapter 3
Up and Away

Billy *rushed* over to the magician. He had to get Fang-Face back. But Jack's mom was making everyone go outside.

Time for the treasure hunt in the backyard.

There was nothing Billy could do. But then, outside, he saw…

He had to rescue them.
What if they were…

…eaten by a bird…

…or **swept** out to sea…

…or carried into

OUTER SPACE?

Billy tried catching the balloon,
but he couldn't jump high enough.

He tried spearing the balloon with a stick…

He **missed**.

"This isn't good," thought Billy. Then the wind started to blow harder. He ran this way…

…and that way, chasing the balloon across the yard. But the balloon kept slipping from his grasp.

The balloon was heading
over the fence…
but, at the last moment,
its string caught in a tree.
"Whew!" said Billy.

A very
tall
tree.

"Oh no!" said Billy as he looked
up. There was only
one thing to do.

He took a
deep breath and
began to climb.

By now, a small crowd had gathered beneath him.

"Go, Billy!" cried Jack.

No one's ever made it to the top of that tree before.

Go, Billy!

Billy kept on climbing. Even though the branches were getting very thin…

He reached across for the Mini
Monsters.

That was
fun!

Let's do it
again!

The branch creaked and swayed
in the wind. Billy wondered if
he was going to **FALL**. Slowly,
carefully, he
picked up the
Mini Monsters.

By the time
Billy got back
down, his legs
felt all **wobbly**.

Ruby was watching him very closely. "What's in your hand?" she asked.

"Well, I've got a secret too," said Ruby. "It's small and hairy, but really amazing. I'll tell you mine if you tell me yours."

37

Normally, Billy wasn't interested in Ruby's secrets, but when she said **SMALL AND HAIRY**, he couldn't help wondering if Ruby HAD found a Mini Monster? Were they *all* at the party?

"Okay," he said at last. "Tell me yours first."

I've found a little pink hamster. **WITH WINGS.**

Where is it?

Not telling...

...until you tell me **YOUR** secret.

Ruby's secret sounded a lot like
Peep. Billy *had* to get him back.

"This is a very important secret,"
said Billy. "Here goes."

Chapter 4
Peep the Doll

"Wow!" said Ruby, when Billy had finished telling her his secret.

Is that really true?

Shh!

"You've got little pet monsters that are **ALIVE!**

Can I meet them?"

Billy looked around to make sure no one was watching.

Then he **OPENED** his hand…

Hello!

"WOW!"
said Ruby again,
and she bent
down to give
Captain Snott
a kiss.

He **blushed**.

Then she patted Trumpet
on the head.

"And there are *more* of them?"
Ruby asked excitedly.

Billy nodded. "I need your help finding them. This is what they look like…" He took out a pencil and some paper.

"Ooh!" said Ruby. "The hairy one's my hamster! Follow me!"

"Remember," said Billy, as they went into the house.

No one must realize what we're up to.

We're a team!

Together, they CREPT UPSTAIRS...

ALONG THE HALLWAY...

And into Jack's sister's room.

"In there," whispered Ruby. "In the dollhouse."

Hello, Peep!

"Quick!" Ruby
called through the door.
"Someone's coming."

50

Billy just had time to slip the
Mini Monsters into his cape pocket,
when Jack's mom came
into the room.

What are
you doing
in here?

"I was just showing Billy the
dollhouse," said Ruby. "Billy
loves dollhouses."

Billy nodded.

Jack's mom looked **SUSPICIOUS**.

Billy looked at the cake table
and groaned. "And I think it's
about to get worse…"

A little while earlier...

Oooh! Yummy!

54

55

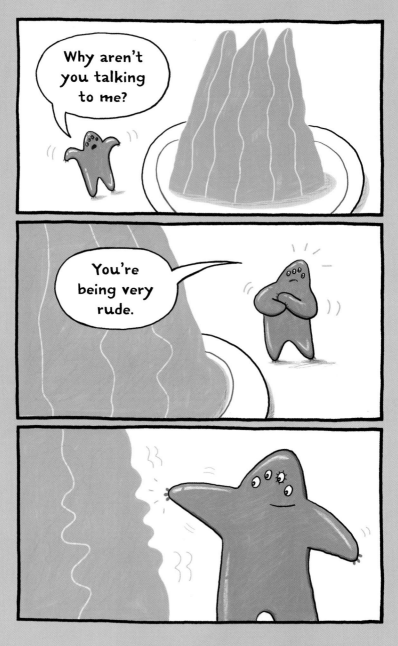

56

Chapter 5
Gelatin and Cake

"Oh no!" thought Billy.
  He could see Gloop on
the table

pretending

to be

gelatin.

He was very good at it.

So good, that if he wasn't careful,
someone was going to **EAT HIM**.

58

But before Billy could grab Gloop, all the other kids started coming in to eat.

Just then, Jack came forward. He was headed for

THE GELATIN.

Billy leaned over to pick up
Gloop… but Gloop wouldn't
let go.

Jack reached for the plate… so
Billy picked up the whole gelatin.

Billy was
trying to
move Gloop,
but nothing
was working.

"**Billy**," said Jack's mom
again. "I asked you to put that
gelatin back."

Gloop!
That's not
another monster.
It's food.

I don't
believe
you.

Jack's mom picked up a big spoon. "Oh no!" thought Billy. "She's going to **CUT** Gloop in half!"

"I'll take it," said Ruby, grabbing hold of Gloop and putting him on her plate.

Where are your manners?

"I'm going to have to tell your mother about this…"

Billy looked around and realized the parents were already starting to arrive. And there was his mom, coming into the dining room.

Luckily, at that moment, Jack's dad called, "Get ready for the cake!"

Everyone stopped looking at the gelatin and started singing "Happy Birthday," – except for Captain Snott.

Billy could hear his little voice piping up from inside his cape.

All the children leaned forward
to watch Jack blow out the candles.
Jack took a deep breath and…

Jack's mom **fainted**.
The parents screamed.

In all the confusion, Billy
grabbed Fang-Face and stuffed
him inside his cape.

"That's all of them," Billy
whispered to Ruby.

Party's over.

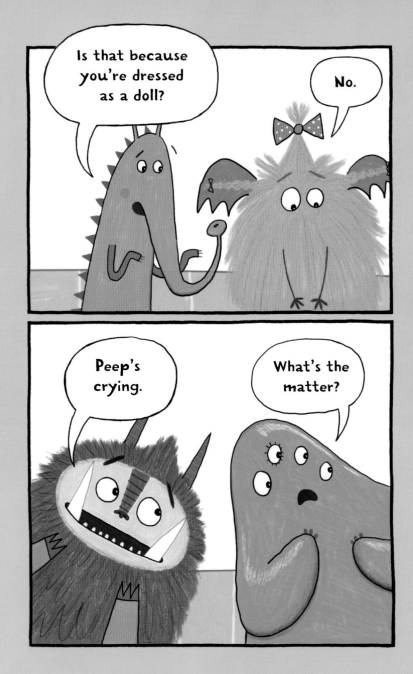

70

Chapter 6
A Monster Party

When Billy and Ruby got home,
their mom

marched

them into the house.

Jack's mom said you had terrible manners!

Why did you both grab the gelatin?

"We're sorry, Mom," said Billy, "but the good news," he added, grinning, "is that Ruby and I are now BEST FRIENDS."

I'm so lucky to have a sister.

I love my brother.

74

As soon as they got upstairs, Billy shut his bedroom door.

"Thanks for all your help today, Ruby," he said. "Maybe little sisters aren't so bad after all."

Ruby grinned.

Shut your eyes, Peep.

"There's something we've got to do…" Billy whispered.

"Happy birthday!" said Billy. "Thank you for being such a great pet monster."

I promise never to call you a hamster again.

TOYS

"Then it really is my BEST birthday ever," said Peep.

All about the
MINI MONSTERS

FANG-FACE →

LIKES EATING:
socks, school ties,
paper, or anything
that comes his way.

SPECIAL SKILL:
has massive fangs.

SCARE FACTOR:
9/10

← **GLOOP**

LIKES EATING: cake.

SPECIAL SKILL:
very stre-e-e-tchy.
Gloop can also swallow
his own eyeballs and
make them reappear on
any part of his body.

SCARE FACTOR:
4/10